_ _ _ _ _ S

_ _ _

_ _ _ _ _ _

_ _ _ _ _ _ _ _ L

Puzzle Contest
PO Box 7877

Burbank CA 91510

June 27, 1989

HAPPY JACK

Weekly Reader Books presents

HAPPY JACK

a folktale retold by

MALCOLM CARRICK

An I CAN READ Book

HARPER & ROW, PUBLISHERS
New York, Hagerstown, San Francisco, London

HAPPY JACK
Copyright © 1979 by Malcolm Carrick
All rights reserved. No part of this book may be used or reproduced in any
manner whatsoever without written permission except in the case of brief quo-
tations embodied in critical articles and reviews. Printed in the United States of
America. For information address Harper & Row, Publishers, Inc., 10 East 53rd
Street, New York, N.Y. 10022. Published simultaneously in Canada by Fitzhenry
& Whiteside Limited, Toronto.
FIRST EDITION

Library of Congress Cataloging in Publication Data
Carrick, Malcolm.
    Happy Jack.

    (An I can read book)
    SUMMARY: Happy Jack bumbles his way into a fortune
and a wife in spite of his stupidity.
    [1. Folklore]   I. Title.
PZ8.1.C2273Hap   [E]   78-19476
ISBN 0-06-021121-0
ISBN 0-06-021122-9 lib. bdg.

For Keli and Nanerl

Jack was happy

and very lazy.

He did not work.

All day he stared

at the faraway sky.

Jack's mother

was very unhappy.

"We have no money left,"

she wailed.

"What shall we do now?"

Happy Jack smiled.

"I will get a job," he said.

"Then we will have

pots of money."

8

Jack went to a farm.

"Can I have a job?"

he asked the farmer.

"Yes," the farmer said.

"You can start on Monday."

So on Monday

Jack started work.

He plowed the fields

in straight lines.

The farmer paid him

for his day's work.

Jack was so happy

he hurried home.

But on the way

he lost his money.

"You should have put your money

IN YOUR POCKET!"

his mother cried.

"Now we have

no money again."

On Tuesday

Jack said to himself,

"Today I must put my pay

in my pocket."

Jack worked very hard.

He milked the cows

and goats

and sheep.

At the end of the day

the farmer gave Jack

a full jug of milk.

Jack remembered what

his mother had told him.

He put the jug

in his pocket.

Jack was so happy

he danced all the way home.

21

"You have spilled all the milk,"

his mother shouted.

"Now we have nothing to drink.

You should have put the jug

ON YOUR HEAD!"

On Wednesday

Jack made cheese.

At the end of the day

the farmer gave Jack

a big runny cheese.

He put it on his head.

"Oh no!" his mother yelled.

"You should have carried the cheese

IN YOUR HANDS!

Now we have nothing to eat."

So on Thursday

Jack said,

"Today I must carry

my pay in my hands."

He worked in the barn

moving the hay.

28

At the end of the day

the farmer gave him

a laying hen.

Jack carried it home

in his hands.

Jack was pecked all over.

"You fool," his mother moaned,

"The hen has run away.

You should have led it

ON A STRING!

Now we will have no eggs."

On Friday

Jack helped the farmer's wife.

At the end of the day

she gave Jack a ham.

He tied it to a string

and led it home.

"The ham is ruined,"

his mother sobbed.

"You should have carried it

ON YOUR BACK!

Now we have no ham,

no eggs, no cheese, no milk

and NO MONEY!"

By Saturday

Jack was tired of work.

"Today I must carry

my pay on my back,"

he sighed.

"Today we are going to market,"

the farmer told Jack.

The farmer rode to market

on his old donkey.

Jack carried the milk and cheese.

On the way they passed

the mayor's house.

The mayor was very rich.

"Look at those men, Jack,"

said the farmer.

"They are painting."

43

"Why are they painting

each other?"

Jack asked the mayor.

"They are trying

to make my daughter Jill laugh,"

the mayor said.

Jack saw Jill.

"She looks so sad,"

Jack said.

'I will make her happy."

47

"If you do," the mayor said,

"I will give you

pots and pots of money."

"Jack!" shouted the farmer.

"We are late for the market."

All day Jack thought about Jill.

At the end of the day

the farmer said,

"We have done well.

I have enough money

for a new horse.

So you can have the donkey

for your pay.

I don't need you anymore.

Good luck, Jack."

"Good-bye!" said Jack.

He took the donkey home

the way his mother had told him to.

He passed the mayor's house.

Sad Jill saw him

stagger by.

"Oh Jack," Jill laughed,

"you look so funny."

"You would too,"

Jack said,

"if you carried a donkey

on your back."

Jill ran outside.

She hugged and kissed him.

She was happy.

That made Jack happy too.

The mayor said,

"Why don't you get married

and be happy always?"

And so everyone was...

HAPPY.